THE RETURN TO NARNIA
The Rescue of Prince Caspian

BASED ON *PRINCE CASPIAN* BY

C. S. LEWIS

ILLUSTRATED BY

MATTHEW S. ARMSTRONG

HarperCollins *Children's Books*

To Claire –
thanks for all the dandelions
– M.S.A.

NARNIA®

Typography by Matt Adamec   www.narnia.com   1 3 5 7 9 10 8 6 4 2   ISBN-13: 978-0-00-724187-3   ISBN-10: 0-00-724187-9

ONCE FOUR CHILDREN named Peter, Susan, Edmund and Lucy walked through a magic wardrobe into a land called Narnia. They had wonderful adventures there and became great Kings and Queens. But after ruling in the castle of Cair Paravel, they came back home to England.

That was a year ago. Now they sat in a railway station, sad and gloomy because they were on their way to school. Suddenly, they felt a tugging and pulling. "Look sharp!" Edmund shouted. "This feels like *magic!*"

Then the station disappeared and they found themselves in a wood.

"Can we possibly be back in Narnia?" asked Lucy.

"We could be anywhere," said Peter, as they set off to explore.

They walked and walked until they came to an old, broken-down castle. "It gives me a strange feeling," said Lucy.

When Susan found a golden chessman just like one they used to have in Narnia, Peter cried, "These ruins must be Cair Paravel itself!"

"Let's find out," said Edmund.

What had happened in Narnia while they were gone?

Peter led them down some deep, dark steps. "Cheer up!" he said. "If this is Narnia, we're Kings and Queens here, not kids." Sure enough, they found a room filled with treasure – Lucy's magic cordial and dagger, Peter's weapons and Susan's bow and arrows.

"My horn is missing," said Susan. "Where could it be?"

They wondered what – or who – had brought them back to Narnia.

The next morning they met a dwarf named Trumpkin who told them that Caspian, the true King of Narnia, needed help. His uncle Miraz had stolen the throne, and now Narnia was not free. The trees did not walk; the animals did not talk. No one remembered how four children had once helped save the land from the White Witch. And the Great Lion, Aslan, had not been seen for a very long time.

So Caspian fled, planning to raise an army to fight Miraz. He took only one
treasure from the palace – Queen Susan's horn.

Caspian rode all night and all day until he found an army of old Narnians in hiding. There were Badgers, Giants, Fauns, Centaurs and the valiant chief Mouse, Reepicheep.

"Long live King Caspian," they cheered.

When the two armies met on the hill called Aslan's How, the battle went poorly for Caspian. That's when he blew the horn, hoping High King Peter, King Edmund and Queens Susan and Lucy would return.

"It was your horn, Su, that pulled us back to Narnia yesterday!" said Peter.

"No offence," said Trumpkin, "but we were expecting great warriors, not children."

But when Edmund beat him in a fencing match and Susan outshot him with her bow and arrows, Trumpkin believed that they could help save Narnia.

"We must join Prince Caspian at once," said Peter. Together they set off for Aslan's How.

They went to sleep that night hoping they could find Caspian in time.

Later, as Lucy crept into the woods, the forest seemed almost alive. "Oh, Trees, wake!" she called out. "Don't you remember me?" When Lucy was last in Narnia, the Trees talked to her. But this time nothing happened.

The next morning they came to a wild gorge. "We're lost," said Peter.

"No, look," cried Lucy. "There's Aslan! He wants us to follow him." But no one else could see the Lion, so they went another way, no matter what Lucy said.

They didn't get very far before the path was blocked. As they turned back, Edmund said, "Lu, you're a hero for not saying 'I told you so!'"

That night Lucy heard the voice she loved best calling her. She found Aslan among the dancing Trees and ran to him, full of joy. "Welcome, Lucy," the Lion said. "Wake the others now and follow me."

So Lucy led the way, while Trumpkin mumbled about the silliness of following magic lions. Suddenly, Edmund saw a huge shadow. "Oh, Aslan!" he cried.

"Three cheers for Lucy!" said Peter, believing her at last.

At the top of the gorge there was Aslan himself. After greeting each one, he sent the boys and Trumpkin to Caspian but kept Lucy and Susan with him.

The Lion raised his head, shook his mane and roared. The sound rose until it floated over all Narnia, and Lucy and Susan saw a great wave rushing toward them. It was the Trees come to life. They bowed to Aslan and joined in a wild romp. Old Narnia was awake and on the move.

Meanwhile, the boys and Trumpkin arrived at Caspian's camp.

"It's the High King Peter and King Edmund!" Trumpkin announced.

"Your majesties are welcome," said Caspian.

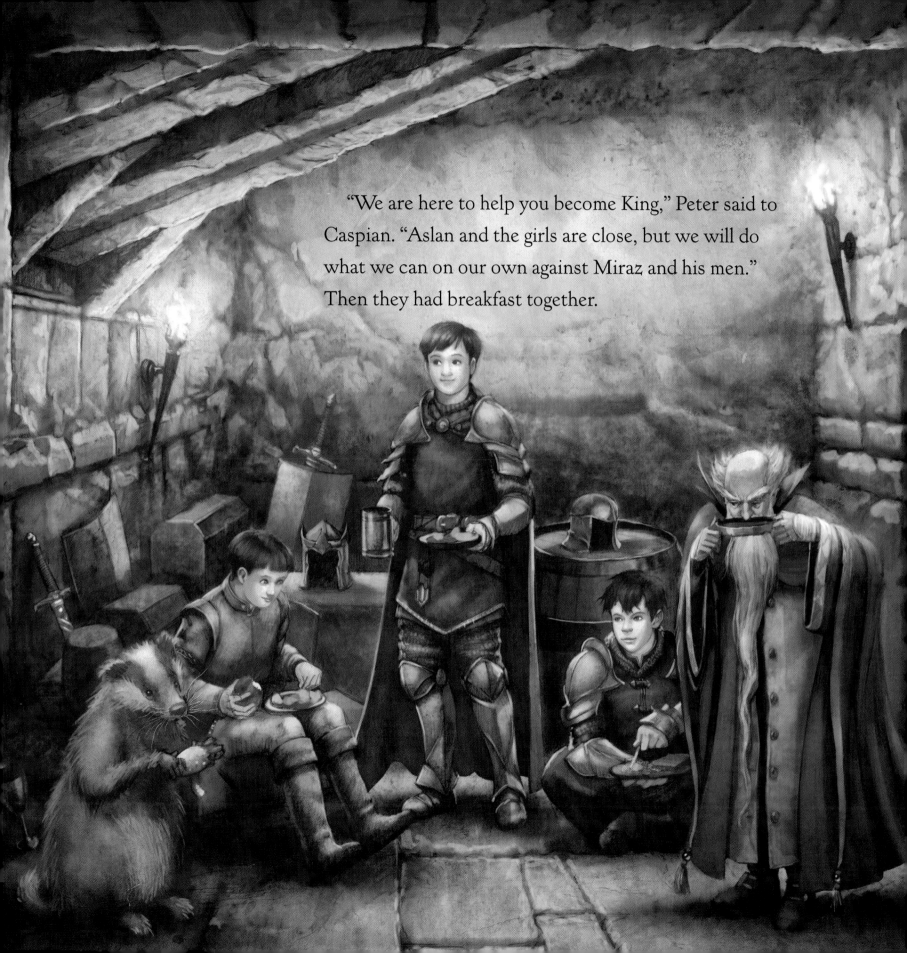

"We are here to help you become King," Peter said to Caspian. "Aslan and the girls are close, but we will do what we can on our own against Miraz and his men." Then they had breakfast together.

The battle began with Peter and Miraz fighting each other. Peter was a great warrior and fought well. When Miraz was betrayed and unexpectedly killed by one of his own men, Peter shouted, "To arms, Narnia!"

"Narnia! Narnia! The Lion!" Edmund shouted as he, too, rushed into battle. Then, with a roar like the ocean, the Trees Aslan had awakened poured over the battlefield. In a few minutes, all Miraz's men had run away.

When Aslan appeared with Susan and Lucy, Caspian knelt and kissed the Lion's paw.

"Prince," said Aslan, "under us and under the High King you shall now be King of Narnia." There was a great feast that night till long after the stars came out.

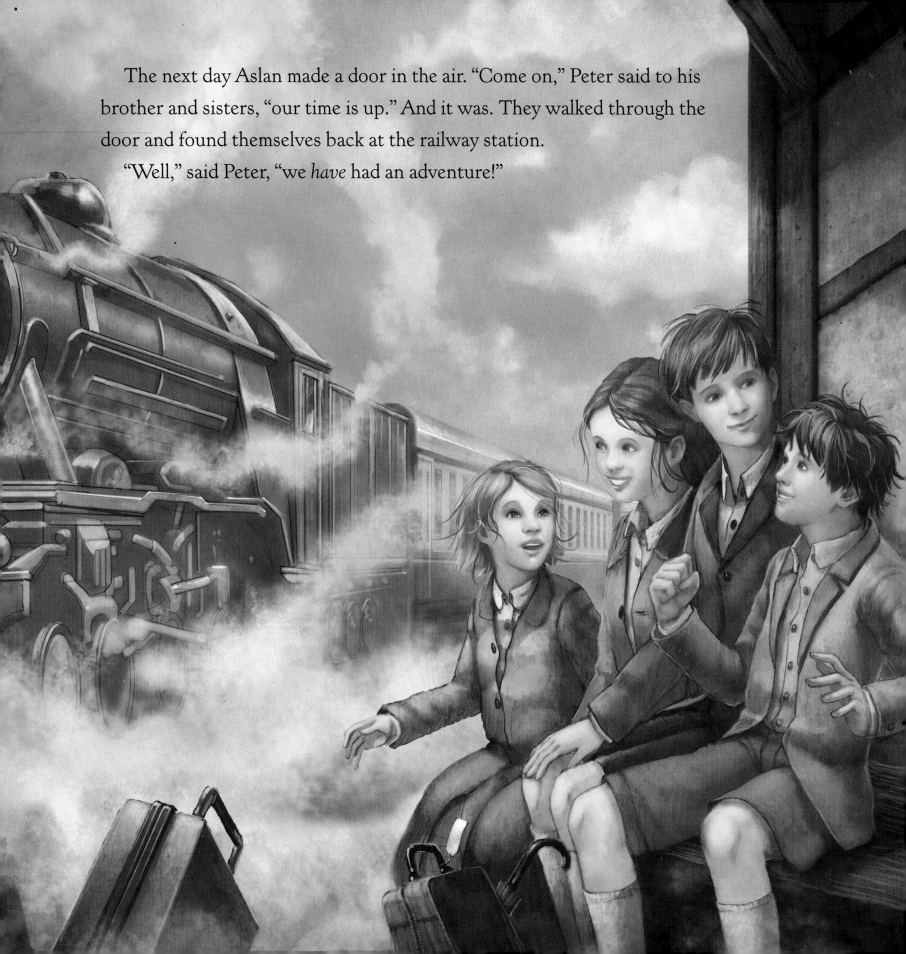

The next day Aslan made a door in the air. "Come on," Peter said to his brother and sisters, "our time is up." And it was. They walked through the door and found themselves back at the railway station.

"Well," said Peter, "we *have* had an adventure!"